XXX SEX STORIES

EXPLICIT DIRTY EROTICA SHORT STORIES

ETHEN SHEAR, JESSICA BANKMAN,CARLEE
SHOMAN,DANIKA FALLS, KELLEN
PRIME,ERIC RESHER,SUSAN STAHLS, TENA
SELDAN, GACY HARPER, KELLIE GRANIER

plicit Press

CHAPTER 1

THE SULTRY SUMMER

TWENTY-NINE-YEAR-OLD LARYSSA BAITS and her twenty-seven-year-old husband, Breckin, had been married for eighteen months when she'd finally agreed to go on vacation. More specifically, she agreed to go camping in a park in upstate New York. No spas or planned activities. Just them, a tent and nature.

On the second day of their vacation, Laryssa was sprawled on the floor of their tent, her long cocoa colored hair fanned out behind her. Her obsidian eyes stared up at the ceiling and she scowled.

"Breckin!" She called. "I'm bored."

A moment later, a pretty-boy face appeared, completed with mussed hazelnut brown hair, indigo eyes, and full lips almost too full for a guy; lips that Laryssa would recognize with her eyes closed. "I think I have something that may cure that."

He stepped inside and, a moment later, Laryssa completely understood what her husband had

.   .   .

meant.

The stranger had thick walnut brown hair that brushed his broad shoulders and light gray eyes that held intelligence that made Laryssa catch her breath. Those eyes widened, then darkened, as they took in her long slender body.

"Laryssa, this is Hollin Amador. He's a bit lost," Breckin sat next to his wife's head and ran his fingers through her hair. "I told him he could crash here with us until we head back down tomorrow."

"That's your wife?" Hollin couldn't seem to stop staring.

Laryssa grinned and ran her hands over her breasts and down her stomach. Breckin and she had been talking about doing this for a while. They hadn't settled anything though, trying to find the right person. Now it looked like the right person had found them.

"Gorgeous, isn't she?" Breckin's voice lowered into the tone that made Laryssa squirm. Her husband looked like the quiet type, but Laryssa knew that when he got that certain quality in his voice, things were going to get a little more interesting.

"I want you to fuck her while I watch," Breckin ran the tip of his index finger along the seam of Laryssa's lips and she flicked out her tongue to caress the pad.

"Are you kidding?" Hollin's words may have been ones of protest, but the growing bulge in his shorts told an entirely different story. His eyes followed Laryssa's hand as it trailed down her stomach, over the dark hair between her legs. She stopped just short of the final goal.

"Touch yourself, Lys," Breckin gave a soft command.

Laryssa kept her eyes on Hollin's ruggedly handsome face as she slipped her fingers between her folds. Her juices were slick on her skin as she slid her two middle fingers into her pussy.

"Talk," Breckin ran the tip of his now damp index finger around Laryssa's nipple. The milk chocolate flesh hardened.

"I'm so wet," Laryssa could hear the breathless note in her voice. She spread her legs further apart and began to work her hand, the heel rubbing on her clit as she plunged her fingers deeper. "I need a cock in me." Even as she said the words, desire for the stranger exploded inside her and she whimpered.

"You're not allowed to cum until I say so," Breckin pinched her nipple and Laryssa cried out, her body tensing as she fought her orgasm. She pulled her fingers from her pussy and Breckin spoke again. "I didn't say you could take your fingers out of your cunt. Keep finger fucking yourself until something else replaces them."

Laryssa whimpered as she slid her fingers back into her pussy. Her body shook as she began a steady rhythm. Her orgasm bubbled just below the surface, every stroke threatening to tip her over, an agonizingly pleasurable torment.

"What do you say, Hollin?" Breckin turned his attention to the stranger, fingers still tight around his wife's nipple. "Want to help her out?"

Whether it was Laryssa's actions or Breckin's words that finally convinced him, he didn't say, but Hollin scrambled out of his clothes, revealing a six feet, a four-inch expanse of toned muscles and golden skin. And a long, thick cock, easily ten inches, curved up towards sculpted abs.

"Damn," Breckin breathed. "You're going to feel that in the morning."

Laryssa didn't respond, too busy wrapping her legs around Hollin's waist as he knelt between her legs. When he finally leaned forward, she grabbed the end of his cock with her hand, slicking the tip of the velvet steel with her own juices.

"Hard and fast," Breckin instructed. "I want her screaming." He glanced at Laryssa. "If you make her cum more than once, you can fuck her as many times as you want, however you want."

Laryssa guided Hollin's cock to her entrance and released him, waiting. "Cum when you're ready, Lys," Breckin nodded at Hollin. "Begin."

The stranger's hips snapped forward and Laryssa's back arched. Her mouth opened in a silent scream, limbs stiffening. He was splitting her in two, stretching her further than she thought possible.

"Oh shit," Hollin panted, eyes squeezed shut for a moment before hooking his arms under Laryssa's legs. He put her ankles on his shoulders and leaned forward, bending her knees back towards her chest.

Laryssa wailed, the sound piercing the forest. Her orgasm had been fading to less intense, softer pleasure. The change in angle gave Hollin a deeper penetration and bumped into the end of her, the combined pleasure and pain immediately sending her body into overload.

Hollin slammed into her, grunting with the force of each thrust and still Breckin urged him to go harder and deeper. Laryssa lost all sense of time, couldn't remember what her life had been like before her body had been riddled with so many sensations, what she'd felt before she had a massive cock filling her, hurting her, pleasuring her. Her synapses were firing and misfiring, her body ablaze.

"I'm gonna..." Hollin started to speak.

"Cum inside her," Breckin was panting and Laryssa knew he had his dick in hand.

Then he tweaked her nipple and she began to sob, no longer aware of him jerking off, of anything other than what was happening to her. It was too much. She could feel the world graying out as her body refused to deal. The last thing she felt before she passed out was the warmth of Hollin emptying himself deep inside her.

Hollin was fucking her again as she floated up out of oblivion. She was on her side as he took her from behind. The face in front of her as she opened her eyes was as familiar as her own.

"Welcome back, Lys," Breckin brushed his lips across hers. "Ready for more?"

CHAPTER 2

THE OLD YEAR PASSES

TWENTY-THREE-YEAR-OLD GENEVIEVE HART had one more New Year's resolution to fulfill and she only had fifteen minutes in which to do it. It was all her best friend's fault. Last year, Genevieve and Jennifer had written each other's resolutions, and, for some reason, Jennifer had decided that her friend needed a bit more excitement in her life, so the final resolution had been straightforward, simple, and insane.

Genevieve had to fuck a total stranger. No exchange of names or numbers. No taking him back to the apartment or going back to his. It had to be completely random and spontaneous. She'd been putting it off for the past twelve months, hoping her friend would forget, but no such luck. Jennifer had called Genevieve twenty minutes ago to provide a delighted reminder.

All of this led up to the paralegal standing in Times Square at eleven forty-give on New Year's Eve, looking for someone to have a quickie with before the countdown hit zero. Genevieve ran a gloved hand through her sienna waves as her shamrock green eyes scanned the crowd. She was pretty, she knew, with one of those baby faces that always made her look younger than she was and curves that made it obvious she was older than her features let on, but she was shy enough that she didn't date much and she never had one-night stands. Which was why, she supposed, Jennifer had done this.

There were so many guys to choose from, of all ages, shapes, and sizes, but her eyes passed over each one. She was looking for something, she just wasn't sure what. It was stupid, she knew. It wasn't like she was ever going to see this guy again, but she just couldn't bring herself to be completely random. There had to be something.

Her eyes met his and she stopped. Mid-twenties, medium height, appeared to be muscular under his coat. Platinum blond hair that gleamed nearly white in the city lights. But it was his eyes that had caught her attention. Even from a distance, she could see the perfect shade of blue-gray, the winter sky over the Northeast just before snowfall.

Before she could talk herself out of it, she took a deep breath and waded through the crowd. He stood at the edge of a group but didn't appear to be part of them. His eyes warmed as she approached, his smile revealing two just-barely-there dimples.

"Hi," his voice was low, cultured, with just a hint of a Boston accent.

"Hi," Genevieve's stomach was in knots. She'd been so focused on finding the guy that she hadn't thought about how to proceed once she found him. He was watching her expectantly, and why not? After all, she was the one who'd sought him out. She blurted out, "I need to have sex."

He started to laugh, the chuckle ending abruptly as he realized she was serious. His eyes widened and Genevieve hurried to explain.

"Last year, my friend wrote my resolutions for me and the last one is to have sex with a stranger."

"And you chose me?" He sounded genuinely curious.

"You have pretty eyes," Genevieve confessed, heat rising to her face. She took a moment to hope he wouldn't notice the difference between the flush of cold and one of embarrassment.

"Do you have...?" His own cheeks reddened.

Genevieve nodded, heart in her throat. She was really going to do this.

The stranger looked around, eyes narrowed as he searched for something that Genevieve couldn't see. He reached down and took her hand, gloved fingers sliding through hers. "This way." He pulled her through the crowd. As the people parted to let them through, Genevieve understood. He'd found a place where they wouldn't be noticed.

A shadowed alcove with a wall of people in front of them, all attention focused on the show. It was perfect. He turned, backing up to the wall. His eyes were glowing with desire and Genevieve had the fleeting wish that she could have met this guy under normal circumstances, and then his arms were around her waist, spinning her so that they were both facing the last band to play before the ball dropped.

Her back was against his chest, layers of fabric preventing them from having any real contact.

She heard the unmistakable sound of a zipper, far louder in her ears than the roar of the millions of people in the streets. Without him needing to ask her, she held the small foil packet over her shoulder. Her hands went to her hips. This was it, she knew, the moment of truth. She had just a few more seconds to make an exit.

Her fingers were nearly numb as she pulled down the back of her sweatpants, taking her panties with them. The wind bit into her bare skin and she shivered. Only half had to do with the cold, a fact she was forced to acknowledge as her pussy grew wet. The soft fabric of a glove caressed one ass cheek and his knee nudged her legs further apart. As she shifted, she felt the head of his cock bump against her and she took a deep breath.

"Are you sure?" His breath was hot against her ear.

Genevieve nodded. One hand moved between them and she felt cold latex against her overheated core. Her eyes fixed on the clock counting down to the New Year and she forced her body to relax. She still couldn't suppress a gasp as he pushed his way inside her. The chill of the latex as it slid inside made her muscles tense involuntarily and she almost told him to stop. She wasn't quite wet enough but he went slow until he was fully sheathed inside her, every inch the pleasurable pain of nearly dry friction.

"Shit, you're hot," he hissed.

She whimpered, needing him to move. Every cell in her body was on edge, waiting for someone to turn around, to notice what they were doing. He swiveled his hips, thrusts shallow, just enough to turn Genevieve's distraction into desire. She pushed her ass back towards him, desperate to finish, partially to avoid being caught, but part of her wanted it now, wanted that release.

"It's almost time," the arm wrapped around her waist snuck under her coat. The people around them started shouting. "Ten... nine..."

His fingers brushed over her belly, feeding the fire there. "Eight... seven... six..."

Genevieve could feel her body responding to the excitement, to the man behind her, and knew she was close.

"Five... four..."

The stranger's hips jerked and the hand on her hip flexed beneath the fabric of his glove. "Three... two..."

She caught her breath as his hand maneuvered beneath the front of her pants, his gloved fingers coming in contact with her clit.

"One!"

Genevieve cried out as she came, her inarticulate sound of pleasure mingling with the revelry of a new year. He followed her over the edge, groaning as he came. His forehead rested against her shoulder as confetti rained down on them. His arm tightened around her waist for a moment before releasing her.

Genevieve straightened, yanking up her pants, face flaming. She was at a loss as to what she should do next. A glance over her shoulder told her that the stranger had discarded the condom with a tissue and was already tucked it back into his jeans. When their eyes met, she swallowed hard. One of Jennifer's requirements had been no names, no numbers. How was she supposed to handle this?

"Same time next year?" He grinned.

She found herself smiling in return. "Sure."

As the new year began, Genevieve watched her stranger disappear into the throng, losing sight of him after just a few feet. She took a deep breath, the brisk air filling her lungs. It was going to be a great year.

CHAPTER 3

THE TIGERS COME AT NIGHT

TWENTY-SIX-YEAR-OLD TAMLYN MOREHOUSE hadn't thought her life would turn out this way. Her rust-colored curls were teased and sprayed into a mass that would last the night. Thick black eyeliner surrounded her jade eyes; heavy green shadow coated her eyelids. Her long legs were encased in teal fishnets, her feet stuffed into knee-high boots with five-inch heels. The leather mini-skirt hugging her thighs stopped just below her cheeks, covering very little of her... assets. Her halter-top left her flat stomach bare and revealed the tops of her 36B breasts, creamy mounds of flesh pushed together to give her more cleavage than she'd ever thought she'd have. Top all of that off with harlot red lipstick and she was ready for work.

The sun had been down for a few hours by the time Tamlyn reached her usual spot. She didn't have to wait long for the first car to pull up to the curb. She bent over, giving the guy inside a nice view.

"Looking for someone?"

. . .

The driver was in his early twenties, hair the color of barley, eyes a lecherous blue-green. He wasn't unattractive, but also wasn't the type of guy girls threw themselves at. "I think I found someone."

Tamlyn resisted the urge to roll her eyes. "What are you in the mood for?" "What's cheap and fast besides you?"

She forced herself to smile. "Fifteen for a hand, twenty for oral, twenty-five if you want me to swallow."

"Get in."

Tamlyn climbed into the Taurus and pointed towards an alley at the end of the block. "We can go there for some privacy."

She was halfway through her night when the rusty Oldsmobile stopped in front of her. The guy inside was in his early thirties, with dark blond hair that looked like it hadn't been washed in a week and muddy brown eyes that crawled over Tamlyn's body. She had the sudden urge to take a shower.

"How much?"

Tamlyn raised an eyebrow. This guy was definitely no stranger to the scene. "What do you

want?"

"Whatever I can get for a hundred," he leaned across the passenger's seat to open the door. "Sounds good to me,"

Tamlyn climbed into the car. She grimaced as the man's hand slid up her

leg, but she didn't make him remove it. "Head up to the alley at the end of the block. We can have some privacy."

"Baby, we're gonna need it," he leered. "I've got something in my pants that's gonna make you scream."

Tamlyn turned her face towards the window, hiding her smirk. If every man who told her that was telling the truth, she would've had a much different life.

Tamlyn sighed as she made her way back up the sidewalk. No matter how many times she did this, she could never get over the sheer exhaustion that filled her by the end of every night. Exhaustion and the tension that had permeated her body ever since she'd started along this career path. She hadn't had a single orgasm in nearly two months, not even a self-induced one.

So when twenty-eight-year-old Cashlin Goodman, an up-and-coming prosecutor Tamlyn had seen around, approached her, how could she say no? With thick copper hair and startling amethyst eyes that couldn't be disguised by the dark of the night, he was one of the most gorgeous men she'd ever seen. When she felt the lean, corded muscles underneath his shirt as he spun them into the alley, she knew this was going to end differently than her prior rendezvous.

She pulled him back into the shadows as his hands moved over her body, setting her skin aflame. "How much for a fuck right here?" His words were hot against her cheek, the wall of the building cool on her back.

Tamlyn's mind reeled as her mouth answered automatically. "Fifty." She barely had the presence of mind to reach into her top and pull out a condom before he was shoving her skirt up around her waist and yanking down her top.

"Fuck," her head fell back against the wall as he ravaged her breasts, hands rough and insistent, mouth greedy. His teeth scraped over her nipples, and his lips pulled the hard pebbles into his mouth. He dropped one hand to free himself and roll the condom over his thick shaft.

Tamlyn cried out as he buried himself in her pussy with one thrust. He was rough and fast, pounding into her with quick, brutal strokes that forced the air from her lungs. She hooked one leg around his waist and gripped his shirt as he rode her. The brick dug into her back but she didn't care.

"You're tight for a pro," he grunted before dropping his face to her neck.

As he sucked the flesh into his mouth, Tamlyn felt her body tip over the edge, months of pent-up frustration exploding into pure ecstasy. Her pussy tightened around his cock and his body stiffened, hips jerking against her as he emptied himself into the condom. She was panting as she lowered her leg, brain desperately trying to make sense of what had happened just in a space of minutes.

"Shit," Cashlin pulled out, hissing as he squeezed off the condom and tossed it to the ground.

With his other hand, he reached into his pocket and withdrew a few bills, his softening cock still hanging out of his pants. "You've got one sweet little pussy there."

Tamlyn blinked, trying to focus. It was only when he reached towards her, money still in hand, that the surreal feeling snapped. She suddenly grinned. As he tucked himself back into his pants, one-handed, she straightened her own clothes. "Why, thank you, counselor." She waited until he took a step back, eyes wide before adding, "I don't believe we've been properly introduced. I'm Tamlyn Morehouse, the newest member of the city's vice squad."

"Oh, fuck," the color drained from Cashlin's face. He started to stammer a denial. "I don't usually do this..."

"Relax," Tamlyn held up a hand. "If I were going to bust, I wouldn't have fucked you."

After a moment, the truth of her statement sunk in and curiosity overrode concern. "I don't understand."

"Let's keep it simple," Tamlyn glanced at her watch. Her shift was almost over and her partners would be looking for her, waiting to see if she'd brought them one last john. "You wanted to fuck, I wanted to fuck. Put the cash back in your pocket and we'll call it... whatever." She started to walk away, stopping when he called after her.

"Think we could... whatever... again?"

Tamlyn didn't look at him, a smile playing over her lips, as she answered. "I'm working again tomorrow night if you'd like to stop by."

She didn't wait to hear his response, just sauntered away into the night, much more relaxed than she'd been in a long time, and with a hint of anticipation in her belly. After all, she had tomorrow to look forward to. Overall, she'd had a productive night.

CHAPTER 4

A DISTANT WOOD

THEY'D CRASHED four weeks ago. Food wasn't a problem. Boredom was. Two weeks in, the survivors began to – for lack of better wording – became friendlier with each other. By week four, everyone had become accustomed to their new arrangements and were slowly forgetting that their lives had ever been anything but this.

Nineteen-year-old Danika Ware had claimed the remaining tail section of the plane. One bat of her nut-brown eyes and a glimpse of her curvy body and the men had agreed. The only other woman survivor, twenty-two-year-old Kamille Ryder hadn't protested. She was quieter, taller, and athletic with long dark red hair and moody blue-green eyes. Most of the men had assumed flirty Danika would be the most adventurous, but Kamille had surprised them all.

Brett Haines had been the most promising defense attorney at his firm before the crash. Now, he was stretched out on the cool floor of the tail, his russet curls damp with sweat, pale green eyes fixed on the burgundy-haired girl riding him, full breasts bouncing with every rise and fall of her hips. She splayed her hands on his muscular chest, each flex of her fingers digging her nails into his tanned flesh and eliciting a gasp from her partner.

"I'm close," Brett gasped, his hands leaving her hips to take her breasts. As his fingers moved over the firm flesh, Danika looked over at the corner, desire coiling in her belly as her eyes met the hunter-green ones of twenty-six-year-old Maddox Remmington.

The one-time bank manager watched with a lust-filled gaze, his hand wrapped around his cock.

His dark hair hung over his forehead, no longer short and neat, and he bit his bottom lip as he stared. Maddox's hips bucked up into his fist, breath coming in pants as he rode the line between maintaining and losing control.

"Shit," Brett groaned as he came, fingers convulsing and squeezing Danika's breasts. Before he'd even begun to come down, Danika was rolling off, Brett's still spurting dick slipping from her cunt. Maddox was out of his corner and between her legs even as Danika reached for him. She raised her hips to meet him and he slid inside. He was bigger than Brett, and Danika made a sound of satisfaction as she stretched to accommodate him.

His first stroke finished what she'd started with Brett and she cried out as she came. Maddox's mouth worked over her nipples, his lips tugging while teeth scraped and she found herself headed towards the cliff again. Pleasure bubbled up inside her as Maddox pounded into her and she arched her back, pushing her breasts further into his mouth. Danika's nails scraped over the back of Maddox's coat, desperate for purchase, for some outlet to the sensations wracking her body. When he hooked her legs over his arms, she squealed, his cock raking over her g-spot. The second stroke sent her over the edge and her body shuddered, muscles squeezing his cock.

"Fuck," he grunted as he came, his hard length pulsing inside her.

And from the other side of the clearing, they heard the familiar and unmistakable sound of Kamille cumming.

As silent as she was normally, when having sex, Kamille was loud and vocal. "Fuck me, Aitan, come on, don't be a pussy. I'm not going to break."

Golden-haired Aitan Merlowe shifted his stance, giving himself the leverage he needed to slam into Kamille's cunt at a brutal, bruising pace. She was bent backward, lower torso in the air, legs nearly behind her head, hands working over the thick, swollen cocks of nineteen-year-old Raj Pittman and twenty-five-year-old Bayron Sinclair.

"Yes," Kamille cried out as she came again. It hadn't been until she'd taken off her clothes that first time that her companions had started to realize that the soft-spoken persona was far from all there was to the first-grade teacher. The small silver rings through both nipples and the elaborate artwork inked over nearly every inch of her upper torso had given her credibility when she'd explained her desire for what most people considered painful.

Now, as Aitan's thick, foot-long shaft repeatedly slammed into her cervix, the pain that came from that contact sparked along her nerves, translating into pleasure that had her convulsing, muscles quivering as she pleaded for more. Aitan bottomed out one final time, swearing as he emptied himself deep inside.

Raj and Bayron each grabbed one of Kamille's hips as Aitan withdrew, easing her to the ground.

Bayron stretched out, his dark blond hair full of debris from the clearing. His dark violet eyes were blown nearly to black as he pulled Kamille on top of him. He and Raj manhandled her into place, his cock – though far from average, still smaller than Aitan – easily sliding into place. He pumped up into her a few times, as Raj positioned himself between Bayron's legs.

"Fuck my ass," Kamille ordered, glancing over her shoulder at the copper-haired teenager. The youngest in the group, Raj had actually been a virgin when the trip began, too shy to approach either of the girls. It had been Kamille who had taken one look at the pretty-boy face and beautiful steel blue eyes and dropped to her knees to give him his first blowjob. He'd since fucked both women, but his preference for Kamille was obvious.

"Gladly," he grinned, running his hand between her legs. Bayron didn't even flinch when the other man's fingers brushed his cock. They'd done this a few times already and knew how it worked. Raj ran his hand over his stiff seven inches, giving himself some lubrication before placing his tip at Kamille's other hole.

"Just shove it in," she writhed on top of Bayron, making him swear. "I'm still stretched from this morning."

Raj did as he was told, his hands on Kamille's slim hips as he pushed past that first ring of muscle. Once the head popped past, he slid the rest of his cock in with little resistance.

"That's it," Kamille hissed, closing her eyes. She let the sensation of fullness, of reaching that point of nearing too much, fill her. The burn in her ass, the throbbing between her legs, all of it took her away from where they were, from what had happened. With the two men fucking her, alternating strokes so that she was never completely empty, she could almost pretend she was back home, ordering her submissive to pleasure her in every way imaginable. She could almost pretend that she'd never left him to go on this stupid business trip.

She preferred these three to the other two. Aitan was so large that he could make her scream like no one else and the two currently on top and underneath her were talkers. The two fucking Danika were far too silent for Kamille's tastes. She wanted to let their words wash over her, fill her mind, and drive away any thoughts of what she'd left behind.

Bayron liked letting her know how she made him feel. "You're so hot and tight, baby. It feels so good inside you."

Raj, on the other hand, ran his mouth like he was auditioning for a phone sex line. "You like that, don't you? You like my dick in your ass, fucking you, while Bayron does your pussy. I can feel him, you know, feel his cock moving inside you."

The man beneath her stiffened.

"Shit, he's cumming," Raj's words were breathless as his hips snapped forward at an increasing pace. "I can feel his dick pulsing in your cunt; can feel his cum shooting inside you."

This was one of the main reasons Raj had become Kamille's favorite partner. His words were liquid sex, hot and sticky, coating her skin. The heated pressure that had been building inside her exploded and she came again, this one harder than the previous two, her entire body tensing, muscles squeezing Raj's cock until he called out her name and came, hips jerking as he emptied himself into her ass.

As night fell for the seventeenth time on the band of survivors, they huddled together for warmth, unsure if the next day would bring rescue or more of the same. One thing they knew, at least they had something to keep them occupied while they waited.

CHAPTER 5

LONG THE WINTER

TWENTY-FOUR-YEAR-OLD ZAHRA PINE swore as she saw the one word she didn't want to see next to her flight: delayed. If it had been canceled, she could've left, but her boss would be furious if she left without waiting out a delay. She twisted her long coffee-colored curls up behind her head, sighed, and pulled her suitcase into the closest lounge. She folded her athletic body into one of the chairs and peered out of the window.

Thick, heavy flakes fell lazily from the black night sky. The roads had been treacherous; her taxi hadn't gone more than a few miles before she was starting to regret not having declined the trip. Her forest green eyes turned from the nasty January weather to the others waiting in the nearly-empty lounge.

There was an older couple chatting quietly, their single suitcase at their feet. A younger couple with a sleeping baby and a mother who looked about ready to join her child. Two men who, based on their suits and briefcases, were headed out for business reasons like her.

Then she saw him. White blond curls, electric blue

eyes, a classically handsome face, and a tall, athletic body under well-fitting jeans and a dark blue sweater. His eyes met hers and lit up. He stood and sauntered towards her with the easy grace of a long-time athlete.

"Leal Bloom," he held out a hand.

"Zahra Pine." The moment his skin came in contact with hers, she shivered, and it had nothing to do with the temperature. Suddenly, the wait ahead didn't seem so bleak.

They were already kissing when they tumbled into the supply closet. They'd been talking for a couple of hours, their bodies leaning closer with each new topic. When Leal's fingertips had brushed over Zahra's cheek, she'd instinctively closed her eyes and then his lips had brushed against hers. It hadn't taken much to go from that to tongues tangling, hands searching for access to the flesh.

Zahra moaned into Leal's mouth as his hands worked their way under her hoodie, his flesh cool against her overheated skin but still burning a trail of fire across her nerves. When she tripped over a box, their mouths parted, both breathless as Leal caught her. They were both laughing as Zahra kicked the box out of the way, her eyes sparkling in the dim light. She grabbed the hem of her shirt and yanked it over her head, heat pooling in her belly at the expression on Leal's face when he saw her dark green bra. She winked. "Care to reciprocate?"

Leal blinked, and then scrambled out of his shirt, tossing the sweater on top of Zahra's hoodie. She made an appreciative sound, reaching for Leal again. She ran her hands over his broad shoulders, down across his muscular chest to his sculpted abs. Her fingers played with the fine curls just under his belly button, following them down to the waistband of his pants. They hung low on his hips, revealing the deep v-grooves that pointed towards the impressive bulge in the front of his jeans. She cupped him, grinning as his hips jerked.

"Mmm," she murmured, looking up at him through her thick lashes. "Is that for me?"

Leal crushed her against him, slanting his mouth over hers, tongue plundering her mouth as his hands roamed the bare expanse of her back. She felt his fingers at the clasp of her bra and moved her torso enough to wiggle free of the garment. He turned them and pressed her back against the door, his hands between their bodies to caress her breasts. When her fingers unbuttoned his jeans and began working at the zipper, he made a noise in the back of his throat and pushed his leg between hers, grinding his hips against her thigh.

"Get these off," she tore her mouth away from his, hands desperate to shed the last of their clothes.

In record time, jeans, boxers, and panties were forgotten on the floor, and their eyes were greedily devouring the newly bared flesh. Zahra was long, strong legs and firm breasts with dark brown nipples. The hair between her legs was sparse and dark, already glistening with moisture from her arousal. Leal was all hard muscle with a trim waist and a path of pale hair leading down to the thick erection curving up from equally pale curls. Easily nine inches, his cock was flushed with blood, pre-cum already leaking from its head.

"I've been hard since the moment your hand touched mine," Leal rolled the condom down his impressive length, eyes flicking up to hers. His pupils were blown wide, only the barest sliver of blue showing.

Zahra put one foot up on the box she'd tripped over and held out a hand. "And I've been wet just as long. Come on."

The smile that curved Leal's lips spoke volumes of desire and lust and want. He stepped up, his eyes met hers as he began to ease his way into her tight, hot channel. His hips made shallow thrusts, each one taking him just a little deeper, sending another thrill through Zahra's body. She fought her impatience, wanting to enjoy every moment. It had been far too long since she'd met someone who knew what they were doing and she had a moment of regret that she and Leal didn't have a long weekend in bed so she could test the extent of his skill.

"You're thinking too much," Leal ran his thumb along her full bottom lip. "I must be doing something wrong." He dropped one hand between their bodies and brushed his thumb over her clit.

Zahra whimpered, body twitching in response to his touch. Leal grinned and gathered her wrists in his other hand, lifting them above her head to rest against the door. Blue locked with green, both full of everything they wanted to say and couldn't say. Leal drove the remaining four inches into Zahra with one thrust, his body flush against hers, mouths mere centimeters apart.

"Fuck," the word was little more than a breath of air. Zahra's breathing stuttered as she stared into Leal's face. She could feel his heart pounding against her chest, feeling each time he inhaled. There was no give behind her, no way for her to escape the sudden intimacy of the situation.

Leal bent his head the small distance needed to bring their lips together, darting out his tongue to trace her lips before parting her lips and penetrating her mouth. The lower half of his body began to mimic the movements of his tongue, thrusting deep inside in a rhythm that had Zahra writhing, her arms pulling against his grip. She wasn't sure if she wanted to pull him closer or push him away, her body on overload as it absorbed the pleasurable friction between her legs. The base of his cock rubbed just right on her clit and she felt herself hurtling towards an orgasm faster than she ever had before.

Then his teeth were tugging on her bottom lip and she was suddenly there, crying her pleasure into his mouth as he worked her through one and into the next, his body dancing against hers.

It wasn't until she came a second time that he released her hands, letting them fall, limp against his shoulders. He pulled her away from the door to wrap his arms around her waist, one hand splayed across the middle of her back, the other cupping one ass cheek to press her hips even closer. His mouth left hers, lips traveling across her jawline and down her neck, even as he never missed a beat. His fingers dug into the flesh of her ass and he buried himself more deeply than before. As his teeth nipped at the tender flesh of her throat, his cock pulsed inside her and she knew he was cumming. The combination sent another ripple of pleasure through Zahra and she clung to him, letting their bodies merge until she wasn't sure where she ended and he began.

"Now boarding for flight 72 to New York."

Leal looked down at Zahra. "That's my flight." He stood, reluctantly releasing her hand. "This

. . .

was…"

"Amazing," Zahra finished the thought as she stood. "If you're ever back here…" She let the invitation hang, unfinished.

"And if you're ever in New York," Leal brushed back a stray curl and sighed. "If I didn't have to work tomorrow, I'd be tempted to stay until your flight leaves."

"I never did ask," Zahra walked with him to the line of people waiting to board. "What do you

do?"

Leal grinned. "I'm a backup dancer on Broadway." Zahra's eyes widened and he laughed. "I know, not what you'd expect." He paused and took her into his arms. His lips were gentle against hers. "I'm serious, by the way. Call me if you're ever in New York. We'll go see a show."

"Or stay in," Zahra winked.

Leal's smile widened. "That's an option too." He released her. "Best wait for a flight that I've ever had."

Zahra nodded in agreement and then watched as he disappeared through the doors. "Flight 175 to Miami will begin boarding in ten minutes."

Zahra reached for her suitcase. It was time to go. It was a shame, though, she thought, that she was heading south. She was beginning to like the snow.

CHAPTER 6

CHRISTMAS CRAVINGS

TOM WALKER SHIVERED as he hailed a cab to downtown New York. It was 6 p.m., a few hours before Christmas Eve. Everything was ready, from the brightly-wrapped gifts, and the sumptuous dinner. He had everything, except for someone with whom he could spend Christmas Eve.

He had always believed in good luck, and he was sure this was one of his lucky days. He drove downtown, parked, and sneaked surreptitiously into the El Grande, a singles bar. He sat in one dark corner of the crowded area. *Surely, I could find someone here*, he thought.

He ordered a martini and watched as some of the revelers danced in the small space at the center of the bar. He was engrossed watching them cavort to the music. He thought it was sexy, and his crotch started to bulge.

He always felt aroused watching people dirty dancing. Just then a hand settled on his lap. He looked up to see a beautiful, female Santa smiling at him.

"May I?" she indicated the vacant chair beside him. "Sure," he grinned back.

He offered her a drink, and they started talking.

"I'm looking for someone to spend Christmas Eve with," Tom frankly revealed. "I have everything ready but no one to share it with."

"Oh," there was a pause. "So here I am. I'm Michelle."

She was already caressing his engorged manhood with her deft fingers.

"Hmmm, it seems, you've not been laid for quite some time," she giggled into his ear.

"Let's go," he pulled her up to her feet and they slinked their way out, his erection unnoticed amidst the cavorting bodies on the dance floor.

Tom was not able to wait any longer. He was so horny; he had to fuck her right then and there. He led her to his parked car and they were at each other even before the car's door was closed.

Hungrily, they sucked each other's lips, the slurping sound clearly audible a few feet away. Michelle impatiently unzipped his jeans to release his rigid cock from its constraints, while Tom had unbuttoned her blouse and was sucking her right nipple and twirling her left nipple with his fingers.

The space in the backseat of the car was just enough for them to be in a sitting position. Michelle had straddled him, the soles of her feet planted firmly on the backseat - one on each of Tom's sides - as she pressed her hot pussy on and off of Tom's glistening penis. The clitoral pressure from his pubis made her mad with lust. They were still half-dressed, but this did not stop them from exploring each other.

Tom nestled his head on her luscious breasts as they came bouncing down from her opened blouse. Their warmth and softness made him hornier. He rammed his dick upwards to meet her slick pussy. Up and down Michelle rode him, her brows gleaming with sweat, her breath coming in rapid spurts, and her face beet red with her incoming orgasm.

Tom felt Michelle's juicy vagina enclosing his shaft in a tight grip, and then sliding in and out of him, in a superb interplay of sensations. The pleasurable friction of his huge dick with Michelle's tight pussy was beyond anything he had ever experienced.

He groaned in utter pleasure as Michelle increased her tempo and slid back and forth on his angry cock.

"Ahhh," he groaned in amazement at the delicious sensations that coursed from his groin to every nerve of his body.

He met her movement with powerful thrusts of his own, the sound of the slapping of their pelvis mixed with their moans of delight revolved around the confines of the car.

Michelle arched her back and locked her pussy onto his manhood as her climax flooded her body, and she convulsed in one humongous climax.

Tom, however, was still hard and unfulfilled. He held her by the waist and brought her down forcefully onto his still upright dick, as he strained to achieve his orgasm. As Tom continued fucking her, she climaxed again; it was even more intense than the first one, leaving her screaming with delight and thrilling pleasure.

Tom climaxed then and held on to his dick as he squirted his creamy, sticky semen onto Michelle's breasts. Michelle reached out to lick the tip of his penis, while Tom savored the heavenly sensation.

They sat there in the backseat for a few minutes looking at each other and smiling impishly. "That was unbeliev-able!" Tom nudged her.

They were still half-naked, spent but fully satiated after their fiery intercourse. Michelle's Santa hat and Jingle bells were half-strewn in the front seat.

"C'mon, let's get home and celebrate Christmas together."

They arrived at Tom's house a few minutes before twelve midnight. They dined and wined until they got drunk and started to get horny again.

"Will you stay here longer?" Tom asked her as he knelt to kiss her pussy.

"Yes, I want that," Michelle crooned as Tom pushed her to the wall and raised one of her legs to expose her swollen clitoris. "Mmmmm, I like that very much," she exclaimed as Tom's tongue flicked her clit in deliberate but gentle strokes.

Michelle grabbed a handful of Tom's hair as he parted her labia and his tongue entered her pussy to explore it. *Ahhhh, such exquisite pleasures*, she thought. She played with her tits as Tom devoured her pussy, licking her labia up and down, and then sucking her clit relentlessly until she whimpered exultantly.

She wanted both of them to climax simultaneously, so she knelt in turn, and took his penis into her hands, massaging it gently, as it grew even bigger. She ran her tongue around the crown of his penis, sucking softly as her fingers massaged his shaft in upward and downward motions.

Tom closed his eyes and raised his head in pure delight as the incredible sensations overcame him. Then Michelle ran her tongue up and down his shaft, and round again his crown as he, in turn, clutched her hair and prodded her to take him fully in her mouth.

Michelle did so happily, and soon her tempo quickened and her mouth moved in and out of Tom's manhood as he groaned with desire at her ministrations.

As her mouth moved in and out of his dick, her fingers were also massaging the base of his penis, in matching tempo with her lips. She went on, keeping the rhythm until he grunted and climaxed into her waiting mouth.

As Tom basked in the delight of his orgasm, he was sure the days ahead would be as exciting as that Christmas Eve.

CHAPTER 7

EURO TRASH PARTY FUCK

NAKED, Cindy said, "Max enough fucking. I want to go out tonight!" "That sounds demanding!"

"You said I could have anything I wanted when we started swinging."

"Like I'm the only one who likes to fuck others," Max chortle loud. He hopped out of the bed and put on his red robe. He slipped his Hawaiian shorts over his cock. A drop of sexy Asian girly oil clung to the hung dick of Max. Even soft, he was about six inches long!

Cindy rolled over on her tummy flashing her plump ass cheeks. She knew Max never put up much resistance upon seeing her yellow Asian ass. "I finished my Yacht collection in the den. Now is time for a new project. Or," she paused and bit her lower lip and pouted. "An old project we both enjoyed so much."

. . .

"And what is that, Tiger Pussy," Max said, squatting beside the bed and looking into the pretty slanted grey eyes of his wife.

Cindy's own grey Asian eyes looked at him. "There's a Euro Trash Rave Party downtown. They throw them for the EU models so they don't feel lonely in the states."

"My cock's not getting hard," Max said and got up and closed his robe over his grey chest hairs. He tied the red robe. "But we never know what or more specifically whom we may find. How many people do we have in our Professional Swing set?"

Excited Cindy sat up and threw her little legs over the bed. She was only five-foot-three inches tall. Her blue bob haircut always attracted one dick, cock or dong or another. "There you and me, 2, Clarissa and Hans, 4."

"Not nearly enough. I'm in the game. Let's go!"

Cindy loved loud Rave parties. She met Max at an outdoor loud classical music festival four years ago. Now they're happily married for four years. To keep their marriage happy, Max introduced Cindy to swinging. Cindy loves it. She feels like a whore sometimes. But sometimes she wants to feel like a whore. She was the only Chinese girl child given up for adoption thirty years ago. They took a few drinks and started casting their eyes about the writhing male and female flesh.

. . .

"How about those two over there," Cindy nodded with her small round head. Cindy's blue eye shadow and slight blush and bronzer made her look almost European under the party lights. The woman Cindy liked had crescent-shaped eyes.

"Wow! She's pretty. Class for a Euro Trash!"

Cindy ruthlessly mocked Max. "He's handsome and that package's got to be at least eight- inches."

"All about the size."

"What else can a horny girl care about?"

Cindy and Max danced their way over only to have the couple leave the floor.

"Plan B," said Max undisturbed.

The couple settled down by the bar for drinks. No empty seats flanked them. Cindy held Max's hand. "If the sun is supposed to rise--it will."

"I've been meaning to ask you about that quote you keep saying," Max finally questioned. Cindy gave him a conspirator's look. She smiled. "It means fate. Luck." She nodded. Two empty seats opened up one on either side of the Euro couple.

The woman wore a tight black mini dress. He had brunette hair. Her biscuit-colored white skin threw her empire cone-high ponytail into the spotlight. She had powder blue eyes. Gold pearls around her neck and a few wrists candy bracelets that sparkled against the liquor bottles and bar light. The man wore black pants, nice dress shoes, and a white T-shirt that looked formal. Black blazer. He had a pencil-thin dark mustache and a rectangular tuft of chin hair. His cobalt eyes hinted at annoyance.

"Hello," said Max to the woman. "We admired your dancing. You two been together long?" The young Euro Trash model perked up, as if glad, "No. Tajh and I. I'm Dejah . . ." She paused to shake Max's hand.

Max immediately noticed her leopard fingernail polish. "No, we've been together only a year. We model clothes."

Cindy sat down next to the man. "I admire a man who has the courage to wear his style. The mustache and beard don't exactly match. On you, however," Cindy smiled and lowered her eyes bashfully, "It looks down right manly."

The Euro guy sat up straighter in his chair. He turned his attention squarely to Cindy and soon they moved out to the dance floor.

The woman projected confidence. "I'm glad you showed up. Nothing can be more boring than staying with the same person all the time." She picked up her Shirley Temple.

Max ordered a Brandy Sling for himself. "A toast to meeting different people." The two clanked their glasses.

"You know, me and Cindy are swingers. We're professionals though. We don't--" Max paused to let the professional sink into Dejah's pretty ears. "Just let anyone in." He took another drink from his Brandy Sling. "You want to join us?"

. . .

She turned to see, Cindy and Tejh dancing very close. "Why not?"

Max's head motioned sideways towards Cindy and Tejh. "Come. Let's tell them."

Cindy said excitedly, "Tejh wants to see our penthouse apartment, Max!" Max replied, "Great." He smiled at Dejah.

She smiled back.

"We'll follow in our car," said Dejah. The younger dark-haired couple went to their modest Volkswagen car and followed Cindy and Max in their grey BMW.

"I like the entertainment center," Dejah remarked.

"You haven't seen it playing porno DVDs yet." Cindy chuckled, holding Tejh's hand and guiding him into the bedroom. Soon Tejh's eyes clenched tight as Cindy rode up and down his eight-inch thick cock. That fucking cock speared Cindy's cooze breadth-wise. Cindy crotched over his stretched-out thighs. Her butthole was clearly visible and puckering as she pushed off Tejh's strong, hairless chest. Cindy cowgirl humped him up and down and her pussy made loud "Plop, plop, plop" fuck sounds.

Max hugged the shocked Dejah around her slender 25-inch waist. Her figure was of a lipstick lesbian, all smooth, graceful perfectly proportioned in every way. "How about we fuck in here on the couch." Max bit her earlobe lightly.

. . .

Soon Max had Dejah's legs crossed at the ankles over his shoulder. Her Euro-biscuit white fingers pried open her rosy pussy snatch. Her meaty pussy shocked Max. He thought he'd seen it all. "I just want to eat your snatch. You're so full down below."

Dejah grinned. That was all she needed. "Tejh never wanted to eat my pussy."

Max countered Tejh's thoughts, "When you're a young man, sometimes you don't know a good meal when you see it."

Max and Dejah fucked with their eyes open. Dejah licked her burgundy lipstick. She tossed her head side to side as Max plundered her fuck space. Her juices ran down her pussy, past her asshole, and onto the couch. Naked Dejah grunted loudly. She didn't hide the exquisite pleasure Max drilled into her hot fuck core. She slicked up her fingers in her fuck juices and rolled Max's big balls shamelessly in her hands before saying. "I want to suck your balls before we leave." "We'll do a 69 next!"

Dejah's passion rose to the breaking point. She locked her forearms behind her knees. "I fuck better at swing sessions," Dejah blurted out, "Fuck me like I'm your slave!"

Max relaxed as Dejah's crossed-ankle legs rose high, straight up in the air. He had room to spare and fucked her hard. Max pounded her pussy mercilessly until they both came.

. . .

When Cindy and Tejh reemerged from the bedroom. Max and Dejah sat laughing entangled naked on the couch.

"How about another dance," Cindy said. She moved over to put on the latest rave dance record in their sound-proof penthouse apartment.

CHAPTER 8

HER CHOCOLATE COWBOY

JEROME STRADDLED the horse next to hers and before long, they were riding along the trail behind her father's estate. As Rose looked over at Jerome, she blushed nervously; this was only the third date with this handsome young cowboy from next door. She loved the way he maintained control of his horse, talking to the animal occasionally as they went along.

It was a beautiful morning in Southern Alberta and the view of the Rock Mountains ahead made their little date all the more interesting. They soon got to the huge clearing where they'd planned to have their little picnic. Rose slowly dismounted her horse and tied it to a tree a short distance from where she set the large towel for their food. She made them her famous homemade chocolate-filled croissants. The aroma of the melted chocolate seemed to feel the air. For some reason, Rose had a strong liking for all things chocolate, including her men. Jerome had a smooth dark chocolate complexion that seemed to make her like him even more.

Jerome sat next to her, removing the cowboy hat that he'd been wearing and placing it on the grass next to him. They seemed to thoroughly enjoy each other's company while enjoying the delicious croissants that she'd baked them.

Rose decided to let Jerome in on the fact that she had a crush on him from the first time she saw him. She complimented him on his good looks, to which he smiled and gave her some kind compliments in return. As they continued chatting, it became more and more apparent that they had a deep connection. Slowly she could see him narrowing the distance between them.

She'd tried to convince herself that she wouldn't have anything more than a kiss with him until their fifth or sixth date. But her little pep talks to herself this morning before leaving the house seemed to be useless at this point. She could feel her desire for him growing as the warmth of his lean, muscular body drew closer and closer to her.

Finally Rose gave in to her desires – turning around slightly, she locked lips with Jerome. He didn't resist her, his tongue danced with hers in the ecstasy of the moment. As they kissed, she stroked his impressively lean torso, working his way down to the bulge in the crotch of his pants.

"Go ahead, taste it." With that, he slowly unzipped his pants and pulled out the longest, thickest shaft she'd ever seen.

Rose yelped, as she took him in her hand, carefully scrutinizing his full length.

Jerome gave her a wicked little smile as he parted his legs and allowed her complete access to his manhood to do whatever she wanted. Rose happily welcomed his gesture, bringing her wanton lips down to meet his manhood. As she took him into her mouth, he let out a long outstretched groan.

Rose took his groan as motivation and began working her tongue along his shaft repeatedly. When she got to the head of his shaft, she flicked her tongue over and around the rim, bringing him almost to the brink of his ecstasy. Jerome began slowly thrusting his shaft into her mouth. Over and over, he served her with several hard thrusts, each time his shaft seemed to be going deeper into her mouth. She pulled away finally after almost gagging.

Holding his massive erection in her hand, she carefully scrutinized every inch of his manhood before taking it into her mouth yet again. This time she sucked him hard and fast until he finally pulled his shaft out of her mouth fearing that he'd not be allowed the opportunity to penetrate her core if he ejaculated in her mouth.

Jerome helped her out of her jeans and the underwear that she had on. Then she lay on the grass with her gaze facing the beautiful blue skies. He quickly mounted her and slowly penetrated her moist core with his massive cock. His cock throbbed viciously as he gave her a hard thrust that sent tiny spasms shooting through her entire body. Slowly he began moving his pelvis, thrusting his shaft in and out of her moist core.

Rose felt his cock almost unbearable in length and thickness. Her tight pussy seemed to be stretching beyond its limits to accommodate his full length. Burying himself to the hilt Jerome let out several loud groans, as sensations gripped his body. He began moving faster and faster, slamming his shaft into her wetness, without mercy.

Her high-pitched cries became louder, as he stuffed her pussy relentlessly with his cock. Over and over, he plunged his cock into her wetness. Waves of pleasure come crashing down into her moist heat.

He pulled away and instructed her to get on all fours. As she went down on her knees, she pushed her ass out to face him. A loud smack could be heard as he opened and made contact with her firmly rounded bum. Gripping onto her ass firmly Jerome brings his shaft to the slit of her pussy from behind. Slowly he pushed his manhood into her wetness while gripping onto her.

A loud moan escaped Rose's lips as he continued to penetrate her core. He began moving rhythmically into her wetness until she begged him to fuck her harder. He happily obliged and serves her with a series of quick hard thrusts that sent her body spiraling over the edge.

As he plowed her from behind the sight of two people coming in the distance catches her attention. A voice in the back of her mind tells her to alert Jerome about the visitors so they can stop, but another voice, the more dominant voice, aches, for her orgasm. If she tells Jerome about the two people and he stops, she may miss out on what may be the best orgasm of her life. And so Rose decides to remain quiet about the people in the distance.

Instead, she closes her eyes and grips onto the grass, allowing him to penetrate her core with fury. Each thrust is harder than the last. With a loud ecstatic cry, Rose reaches her climax.

Jerome is pleased with him and increases the momentum of his thrusts.

Suddenly he lets out a loud groan and whips his cock out of her. His juices squirt out of his staff and cover her back nicely.

"Hey, what are you guys doing over there?" a voice calls out.

Rose recognizes the voice, it's her father. Without thinking twice she immediately grabs her clothes and runs, with Jerome following closely behind her.

CHAPTER 9

TEACHERS PET: TABOO

KALEEN COULD NOT KEEP her eyes off of her Spanish professor, Mr. Rosenthal. She loved how his well-defined chiseled body was visible through the light airy white dress shirts that he wore with his black business suit. God, his suit pants did not leave much for the imagination. She had to admit she loved it when he would take the time to work with her on her homework.

Often the thought of being alone with him and what she would love to do to him distracted her while she was in class. She even imagined what it would be like for him to make love to her on his mahogany desk with her legs wrapped around his waist as he began to penetrate her womanly core.

Kaleen could feel the heat rising into her cheeks.

She could smell patchouli oil in the air when she entered his classroom. It was a major turn-on for her. Today she noticed that he would glance in her general direction and then go back to doing what he was for a few minutes, and then when he thought she was not watching he would watch her again. Kaleen could see that he was imagining something, especially when he would lick his lips, but what was it that he was thinking about?

"Kaleen, are you done with the lesson, or is there something that you are having a problem with?"

Kaleen had not realized that she had spaced out. Was she daydreaming that Mr. Rosenthal had been watching her? Pausing to look down at her paper, she realized that she was stuck. She had regretted taking off the time to take care of her father when he was sick the last part of the semester, she was just glad that Mr. Rosenthal was willing to work with her instead of dropping her.

"There were a few issues that I am having with the lesson." Walking up to his antique thick mahogany desk she leaned down and put her book on his desk. She was becoming aroused even more being closer to him. She could feel the heat radiating off of him. She knew that one way or another she needed to keep her cool not letting on that she was turned on by him. Looking over the lesson that she was having issues with he smiled at her.

"Okay, Kaleen in this section it is all about the pronunciation and rolling your R's." As he continued to explain the lesson a little more he could see that she was having trouble concentrating.

"Kaleen, why don't we continue this tomorrow? Smiling up at her, he could not help but notice her ample breasts that peeked out of her baby blue low cut V- neck. He licked his lips looking in to her eyes.

"We can have a study session, that way you can get my undivided attention and there will be no outside inter-ference. "

Kaleen smiled at the idea of having him all to herself. Then she remembered that she was not going to be home. She had promised her mother that she would be home this weekend to get ready for the holidays.

"Sir, is there a way that we can do some studying tonight? I am going to help my mother during the holidays."

"Sure, we can do that. But please call me Eric. Why don't we meet at the café on 1 3 and Grand, say around 6pm? "

He loved that light blue top and the little tan skirt that she wore with the tan 3" inch heels. He wanted to bend her over the desk and take her there but he knew that it was wrong as long as she was a student. It was Taboo. He could tell that Kaleen felt the same way; he had been watching her all semester long.

"That sounds great I will meet you there thank you."

Turning to walk away Kaleen could feel the heat of his stare on her body. She could tell that he was into her and she was going to use that to his advantage. She began to swish her hips back and forth a little more to make her ass jiggle. She knew that it would not only get to him but make him want her even more. Kaleen could not wait for tonight, with any luck there would be more than just studying going on.

When she got home, her heart was racing she felt like she was in high school again going on a date with one of the popular guys in the school. She had to keep in mind that no matter what Eric was one of her instructors and she could get into some serious trouble.

While driving home she thought about tonight and what could transpire. Pulling into the driveway, she looked at the clock. It was 5:15pm. Smiling, she knew exactly what she was going to wear. Once she opened the door, she ran to the bedroom taking out a simple black skirt and a lacy black top with a red camisole to go underneath. Glad that she still had her nylons on she put on her red stilettos and went in to fix her hair. Putting her hair up in a clip she put on some of her Vanilla Musk spray, she took a deep breath. One way or another she had a feeling tonight was going to change her life forever.

Arriving at the café, she saw him right away. Walking up to the table, he pulled her seat out for her. Setting her book down at her place setting, she sat down.

"Thank you for meeting me tonight there are just a few things I need clarification on."

She showed him where she was having issues and as he looked it over, she began to run her leg up against his in a seductive manner.

He looked into her bright blue eyes he knew what he was about to do was wrong but he could not help himself. He had to have her now. Kaleen knew she had him with a small smiling gesture they hurried out of the café and he followed her to her house where they both ran up the porch. As she unlocked the door, she opened it, leading him to her room. He began to run his hands over her body.

"My God you are beautiful."

Taking her clip out of her hair and letting it fall around her face, he ran his hand down to her neck and then down to her ample breasts; he really loved how they felt. Bending down he put his mouth on her nipple suckling it gently. Kaleen began to take his jacket off when he stopped her.

"Let me."

Without another word, he threw his jacket and pants to the floor leaving just his white shirt, which he tore to get it off. Taking his time with her, he led her to her bed lying her down. Looking into her eyes, he could see the insatiable desire that she was feeling. He could tell that she had not been with a man in quite some time when he brushed his cock against her most sensitive part she jumped.

"Are you sure you want to do this?"

Her face flushed, and she looked up into his dark brown eyes. "Yes, I do. I need you more than you know." Arching her hips to meet his she began to run her hands over his bare muscular chest. He was a true masterpiece, everything about him was perfect. Slowly he began to enter her, trying not to harm her in any way. Once her body had adjusted to his large cock he began to pick up the pace he could feel her tighten up around his cock. Damn, he knew it was wrong but he did not care he had to have her. Then he heard what he thought was a gasp "Oh, Eric. Yes. Harder baby"

Kaleen arched her body upwards more so that Eric could suckle on her perky nipples. Then, without warning, Eric flipped onto his back letting her ride, while he ran his hands over her body playing with her full breasts. When he knew that, she getting close to climaxing he made sure to speed up enough that they came together as she collapsed into his arms. Both looked at each other smiling, they both knew that this would not be the last time they would be together.

ABOUT THE AUTHOR

Ethen Shear is an emerging erotica author of many erotica kinks and sub-genres. Be sure to check out other books and leave a review if this story got you hot!

Visit my blog at Ethen Shear Blog

Join my newsletter for the exclusive Ethen Shear Newsletter

Sign up for Free Stories from Xplicit Press Authors

Xplicit Press Author Updates

Like Xplicit Press on Facebook

Follow Xplicit Press on Twitter

Readers: I want to expand a few of the stories to see where the characters can be explored further. If there are any of the stories that you would like to read more about again, I'd love to hear from you!

Keep In Touch
Ethen Shear
info@ethenshear.com